GREAT ILLUSTRATED CLASSICS

THE LEGEND OF SLEEPY HOLLOW
AND RIP VAN WINKLE

Washington Irving

adapted by
Jack Kelly

Illustrations by
Pablo Marcos

BARONET
B·O·O·K·S

BARONET BOOKS, New York, New York

GREAT ILLUSTRATED CLASSICS

edited by
Joshua E. Hanft

Contents

About the Author

Washington Irving was born in New York City in 1783, the very year that the United States won its independence from Britain. At that time, New York only covered the lower tip of Manhattan. Farther north, young Washington Irving could fish and shoot squirrels.

The youngest of eleven children, Irving was named for George Washington, the country's first president. As a boy, he was always interested in strange stories of phantoms and spirits. With his brothers and sisters, he put on romantic plays at home.

Washington spent time with relatives in Tarrytown, about twenty miles north of the city. He probably heard ghostly tales from the old Dutch families in the area. He came to love the Hudson River Valley and the nearby Catskill Mountains.

When he began writing, Irving used a number of pen names. "Diedrich Knickerbocker" was the supposed teller of "The Legend of Sleepy Hollow" and "Rip Van Winkle," Irving's two most popular tales. They were included in *The Sketch Book*, a volume of stories and essays that made Irving famous. Before that time, American readers had always turned to European authors for their literature.

Irving wrote a comic history of New York, and a biography of George Washington, in addition to many more stories and sketches. The author spent many years in Europe, travelling and writing. Later he came back to America and settled in a house in Tarrytown, not far from Sleepy Hollow itself.

Irving has always been celebrated as the first successful and widely read author from the new United States.

Around the Fire

The Legend Of Sleepy Hollow

1

When the good folk of Sleepy Hollow got together around the fire on dark and windy nights, their talk often turned to a mysterious being who had been seen riding along nearby roads.

"He was a Hessian cavalryman who lost his head in the Revolutionary War," one said. "A cannonball took it clean off."

"He's a ghost, the commander of all the evil

spirits in these parts," another claimed.

Nobody knew for sure. But many a farmer, out late at night, would see this apparition go swooping past—an enormous, terrible figure mounted on a powerful stallion. He was the Headless Horseman!

"His body's buried in the churchyard," said one man, who claimed to be an expert on the subject. "At night he rides out to the battlefield where he was killed to look for his missing head. Toward dawn you'll see him go tearing through the Hollow as fast as he can ride. He has to get back to his grave before daybreak."

One of those who listened most closely to these ghostly tales was Ichabod Crane. Ichabod was the town's schoolmaster, and a man who thought he knew a thing or two about ghosts himself.

Ichabod, indeed, looked something like a crane. He was a tall, lanky young man with long arms and legs, hands that dangled a mile

The Town's Schoolmaster

out of his sleeves, and feet like shovels. His small head was perched on a skinny neck. He had huge ears and a long, pointed nose that made his head seem like a weather vane pointing the direction of the wind. Many said he looked like a scarecrow from some cornfield.

Now, Sleepy Hollow is one of the most peaceful spots in the world. It's a hidden valley along the Hudson River that's just as quiet and drowsy and dreamy as it can possibly be. Some say a German doctor, practiced in witchcraft, put a spell on the Hollow many years ago. Others claim that it was the scene of the powwows of an Indian sorcerer even before Henry Hudson sailed up the river that bears his name.

"This is a haunted spot," an old farmer whispered to Ichabod one night. "The sky is full of meteors and shooting stars. And there's nightmares that will slip into your dreams."

During the day, Ichabod didn't have time to

"This Is a Haunted Spot."

think of ghosts and spirits. He was busy running his little one-room schoolhouse. If you went by on a warm drowsy day you might hear the murmuring voices of his pupils reciting their lessons. Or you might hear the stinging whack of the birch rod as the schoolmaster laid into some misbehaving student.

But Ichabod didn't like having to punish his charges. If the child was weak and cried just to look at the switch, the teacher let him off with a warning. When he had to beat a tough young lad for mischief, Ichabod assured the boy that the lashing was "for your own good."

Ichabod liked his pupils. When school was out, he would even become the companion and playmate of the older boys. And he would sometimes walk the younger ones home, especially if they had a pretty older sister or if their mother happened to be good cook.

He always tried hard to keep on good terms with the families of his pupils. He had no

A Companion and Playmate

choice. His salary was very small, and his appetite was very large.

"What's for dinner?" were often the first words out of Ichabod's mouth. Though skinny, he could swallow a huge meal the way an anaconda snake does.

As part of his pay, he would room and take his meals with the farmers whose children went to his school. He lived with each family for a week, then moved on. Over the year, he made the rounds of the neighborhood, all his belongings tied up in a big cotton handkerchief.

Farmers in those days sometimes thought that schooling cost too much, or that schoolmasters were just lazy drones. To make the burden lighter, and to make himself useful, Ichabod would help his hosts with their chores whenever he could. He helped the farmers to make hay. He lent a hand when they mended their fences, took horses to water, drove cows

Rounds of the Neighborhood

to pasture, and cut wood for the winter fire.

"Let me take care of the little lambs," he would say to the mothers. And he would sit for hours with one child on his knee, at the same time using his foot to rock another in its cradle.

One of Ichabod's great pleasures was to pass long winter evenings sitting by the fire with the farmers' wives as they told tales of ghosts and goblins. They would talk while they spun wool and roasted apples in the fireplace.

"That field down yonder is haunted," someone would say.

"There's a goblin that lives under that bridge," another would claim. "I've seen him with my own eyes."

Ichabod had his own tales to tell. He had read books on witchcraft and could relate stories of omens and the odd sights a person could see in the night. He would tell of the dangers of comets and shooting stars. Sometimes he

Telling Tales of Ghosts and Goblins

would scare those ignorant people by telling them the world actually turned around—and that without knowing it, they spent half their time upside down!

It was pleasant telling these tales while sitting snug in a chimney corner. The room would glow with the heat of the crackling wood fire. And of course no ghost dared to stick his head inside.

But walking home afterwards was another story. Then all the terrors of the fables took form around the timid schoolmaster. Fearful shapes and shadows loomed along his path in the snowy evening. Seeing the light of a distant window, he wished he were back safe inside.

"Oh, keep away from me!" he would exclaim. But it was only a bush covered with snow, not a ghost.

"What was that?" he whispered. But it was merely the sound of his own feet breaking

Fearful Shapes and Shadows

through the snow.

It got so that he dreaded even to look over his shoulder, in case someone was following him. But there was one spirit that Ichabod Crane feared more than any other. It was the one the old farmers' wives called the Galloping Hessian of the Hollow.

Sometimes, very late at night, walking through some dark, shadowy glen, Ichabod would suddenly hear a rushing blast come howling through the trees.

"It's only the wind," he would tell himself. But he could never completely convince himself that it wasn't—the Headless Horseman!

2

In addition to teaching school and helping out around the farms where he lodged, Ichabod Crane was the singing master of the neighborhood. He earned many bright coins by

Singing Master of the Neighborhood

instructing young folks in the singing of hymns.

On Sundays, he was very proud to take his place in front of everyone at church and lead his little group of chosen singers.

"I think," he would confide to his friends afterward, "that our hymns this morning really outshone everything else about the service. Don't you agree?"

Certainly you could hear his voice above everyone else's. It carried half a mile, to the other side of the mill pond. And they say that to this day on a quiet Sunday morning the faint notes of Ichabod Crane's high voice still echo in the air near the old church.

An educated man, Ichabod was a gentleman with tastes and knowledge way beyond what the rough country men could brag of. He proved to be popular with all the girls and women of that rural neighborhood. Whenever he came to visit, they were likely to set out

Popular with All the Girls

extra cakes and candies, and to make use of their best silver teapots.

Ichabod went out of his way to encourage the good opinion of the ladies. He would talk with them after church on Sundays. He would gather grapes for them from the wild vines that overran the surrounding trees. He would recite for their amusement all the sayings carved into the gravestones in the churchyard.

"Here lies my wife, and let her lie," he read. "She's at peace and so am I." And all the ladies would giggle.

He would go walking with a whole group of them down by the mill pond, while the bashful country bumpkins hung back. These young men were shy as sheep, and envied Ichabod's elegance and easy way with the girls.

The ladies thought Ichabod a man of great learning. He read to them from a *History of New England Witchcraft*. Witches and magic were subjects that he believed in most firmly

Shy as Sheep

himself.

Wise and educated as he was, Ichabod still loved weird and unusual tales. Living in Sleepy Hollow whetted his appetite for legends of ghosts. The more wild and strange the story, the more likely he would swallow it.

Often after school he would lie in the clover near the gurgling brook and read for hours about witches and goblins and ghosts. It would already be growing dark by the time he headed for home. Every sound of nature spooked his excited mind. The cooing of a whippoorwill from the hillside, the croak of a tree toad, the hooting of an owl, even the rustling of birds in a bush made Ichabod's hair stand on end.

Fireflies scared him. A beetle might bump into him in the dark and he would jump ten feet, sure that he'd been touched by a witch. The only way he could make it home was to sing his hymns, which he thought would drive away evil spirits—or at least drown out the

Lying in the Clover

noises they made.

"There goes Ichabod Crane," a farmer in Sleepy Hollow would say to his wife as they sat by their house at night. "I hear that scrawny schoolteacher's voice again."

But however many fears and frights came over Ichabod, they were merely the terrors of his own mind. Though he'd seen many specters in the darkness, and even been pursued by the devil in various shapes, daylight always put an end to these evils. His life was actually a safe and pleasant one.

Until one day his path was crossed by a being who has caused more trouble for mortal man than all the ghosts, goblins and witches put together—a woman.

3

"Miss Van Tassel," Ichabod Crane said one evening. "Your voice was just marvelous

Miss Van Tassel

tonight. You are certainly making great progress."

Ichabod had just finished giving his little group of singers their weekly music lesson. Katrina Van Tassel, the young lady he spoke to, looked at him through her eyelashes.

"Thank you, Master Crane," she said. "You are too kind." She threw him a very sweet smile, which he quickly returned.

"Please give my best wishes to your mother and father," Ichabod said, as she started for home.

"I will," answered the girl. "I'm sure they would be happy to have you visit sometime soon."

The schoolmaster's adam's apple moved up and down. He blushed with happiness. He kept staring down the road long after Katrina had disappeared, imagining her in his mind's eye.

"Katrina," he sighed to himself.

"Katrina," He Sighed.

THE LEGEND OF SLEEPY HOLLOW

Katrina Van Tassel was the only child of one of the most prosperous Dutch farmers of those parts. She was plump as a partridge, and as soft and rosy-cheeked as one of her father's luscious peaches. She was famous for her beauty, and just as famous for her family's riches, which she would someday inherit.

Of course, not everyone saw her through rose-colored glasses the way Ichabod did.

"That little snip?" one farmer's wife said of her. "Why, she's a flirt and she's stuck on herself. Just look at the way she dresses."

It was true that Katrina liked to dress up in the bright gold jewelry that her great-grandmother had brought from Europe. Her skirt was shockingly short for those days, all the better to show off the prettiest foot and ankle in the neighborhood.

Ichabod had a soft spot for all women, so it's not surprising that he fell for such a pretty girl as Katrina. Especially when he found out how

Famous for Her Beauty

rich her family was.

"Welcome, schoolmaster," boomed old Baltus Van Tassel, when Ichabod paid the family a visit. "Katrina has spoken very highly of you."

Katrina's father welcomed Ichabod with a hearty slap on the back.

"Sh—she—she has?" Ichabod stammered. "Why, of course she's by far my most talented singing student. Her voice is just like a nightingale's, I declare it is."

"Oh, she's full of stories about you," Van Tassel said. "She says you're the smartest man she ever met."

"Well, I don't know about that." Very pleased with himself, Ichabod looked down at his big feet.

As soon as he had a chance, he also looked all around the Van Tassel farm, which stood in a fine spot on the banks of the Hudson River. The barn was as big as a church, full to overflowing with grain and hay. Rows of plump pi-

A Hearty Slap on the Back

geons cooed from its roof.

Sleek fat hogs were lounging comfortably in their pens, or strolling out now and then to sniff the air. A flock of snow-white geese, along with a squad of ducks, drifted lazily in the pond. Several big turkeys went gobbling around the farmyard as if they owned it.

And to top it off, a magnificent rooster strutted across the yard. He flapped his wings, and crowed with pride and happiness. Then he scratched in the earth to find some grubs for his family of hens and chicks.

"My, what a fine farm you have," Ichabod told Katrina's father. "I can't help admiring all your animals. They're so handsome, so well fed."

In fact, Ichabod's mouth was watering. Everywhere he looked he saw not animals, but food—ham and bacon, beef and sausages. When he looked at the pond, he saw geese in their gravy and ducks swimming in an onion

"What a Fine Farm!"

sauce.

Seeing at the pigs, he imagined them roasted with apples in their mouths. He thought about turkeys stuffed and brown from the oven. He could even see the rooster plucked and cooked, lying on its back and ready to be carved.

"You have a good eye for livestock," said the proud Baltus Van Tassel. "Come into the house. My wife has been dying to meet you."

Everything about the house told Ichabod of the family's wealth. Outside were harnesses and nets for taking loads of fish from the river. Huge bags of wool stood ready to be spun into yarn.

Inside the walls were hung with colorful Indian corn and strings of dried apples and peaches and red peppers.

"This is our best parlor," said Mrs. Van Tassel, proud to show off her home to the schoolmaster. The polished wooden table shone like

"Our Best Parlor"

a mirror. In the corner she opened a cupboard so that Ichabod could admire their treasure of old silver.

When he'd concluded his very pleasant visit, Ichabod headed home on foot, determined that someday these rich fields, these orchards loaded with fruit, would be his.

"Who knows?" he said to himself. "I may even sell everything and invest the money in an enormous piece of land out west. They say that's where fortunes are to be made these days."

Yes, he could see it already. He and the lovely Katrina heading out on a loaded wagon for Tennessee or Kentucky, or lord knows where. He even imagined that they already had a family of children who would go with them.

But it was one thing to imagine himself courting the rich and beautiful girl—and quite another thing to win her heart.

He Could See It Already.

4

Ichabod had heard of the knights of the olden days who went out to defend their ladies. They had to fight giants and dragons, and do battle with sorcerers. Then they had to climb stone walls and break through iron gates into the dungeons where the poor damsels were being held prisoner.

"My task is just as difficult," the schoolmaster said to himself. "I must try to win the heart of the beautiful Katrina. And she's such a fickle girl, forever changing her mind. I never know if she's serious, or only toying with me."

And that wasn't all. Like the knights of old, Ichabod had foes. Not dragons or giants, but flesh and blood rivals. There were many young farm boys who thought they were the ones who should marry the fair Katrina. They were jealous of each other, and especially jealous of an outsider like Ichabod Crane. Ichabod knew

Flesh and Blood Rivals

that they would gang up on him if he tried to woo the girl he loved.

"I'm always ready for a fight!" cried the most frightening of all these rivals. His name was Abraham Van Brunt, but his friends shortened that to Brom. And because he was so strong, so powerfully built, everyone called him "Brom Bones."

Brom was known throughout the country as a hardy young man with dark, curly hair and a handsome face. He was bold and liked his fun.

"You should see him ride a horse," Ichabod's friends whispered to him. "And when he says something, that's it. Nobody dares to question him."

Brom Bones was a rough man, but not a bad-tempered one. He and his friends loved to have fun, and would go around the countryside looking for good times. He would wear a fur cap with a fox tail hanging down.

Brom Bones

"Ay, there goes Brom Bones and his gang!" an old lady would say, when the whoops and cries of the band of ruffians woke her in the night.

When someone played a prank, or a fight broke out, everyone knew Brom Bones was likely to be at the bottom of it.

This rogue had already picked out the girl for him. It was none other than the lovely Katrina Van Tassel. He didn't know much about getting a girl to like him. He was gruff as a bear when he approached her. But she seemed to like him anyway—at least, sometimes.

None of the other rivals for the love of Katrina dared to approach her when Brom Bones came to call at her house. If they saw his horse tied out front, they rode on by. His reputation as a brawler was too fierce.

Ichabod recognized that it would be foolish for him to challenge Brom directly. But he took advantage of his position as Katrina's singing

A Band of Ruffians

teacher. It gave him a perfect excuse for paying attention to her and visiting her at home.

Katrina's parents were glad to have the schoolmaster come by. They indulged their only daughter, and paid little attention when Ichabod and Katrina went out walking around the farm in the evening.

We can't know what it was the two talked about as they walked. But we can be certain that Ichabod used all his learning and charm to try to win the fickle Katrina. And he surely thought that he was making some progress. In fact, he might have imagined that his dream of marrying her and inheriting the Van Tassel riches was about to come true.

The neighbors noticed that Brom Bones's horse was not seen very often tied to the fence outside the Van Tassel home any more.

"That Ichabod Crane had better watch out," they said. "Bones is not a man to cross."

Everyone knew that Brom Bones and Icha-

Out Walking

bod Crane would have to face each other sooner or later. Brom wanted to settle the matter like the knights in armor did, by fighting Ichabod face to face.

"I'll double the schoolmaster up," he said, "and lay him on a shelf in his own schoolhouse."

Well, Ichabod wasn't about to give him the chance to do anything like that. He never let Brom rattle him. He never rose to the challenge of his cruder and stronger rival.

Brom Bones tried to provoke the schoolmaster by playing practical jokes on him. Brom and his friends would come storming past Ichabod's peaceful schoolhouse on their horses. They stopped up the chimney and made the building fill with smoke during singing lessons. They broke into the school at night and turned everything upside down. Ichabod wondered if a group of witches might have had a meeting there.

Turning Everything Upside Down

Always, Brom looked for a chance to embarrass Ichabod when Katrina was around. Once he took a mangy old dog and taught him to whine and howl in a very funny way. He sent this dog to sit outside during singing lessons and howl when he heard Ichabod's voice.

The summer passed, and still the two rivals never fought it out. Now it was a fine autumn afternoon. Ichabod sat at his desk in the school. In the drawers were all those forbidden things he'd taken from his pupils—half-eaten apples, popguns, and many, many paper tossing balls.

His students were hard at work. Ichabod had given one of them a taste of the birch rod not long before, so they were on their best behavior. The schoolroom was peaceful.

But the quiet was soon broken by the arrival of a man riding a wild, half-broken colt. He came clattering up to the school like some important messenger.

Clattering Up to the School

"Master Crane," he announced. "You are invited to a party. It is hoped that you will grace the house with the honor of your honorable presence, most honorable sir."

"A party?" Ichabod said. "But where?"

"A party, a merrymaking, a festive event," said the man, full of his own importance.

"Yes, but who invites me?" the schoolmaster asked again.

"Why, the honorable Master Van Tassel," the messenger announced. "This very evening. At his honorable home. What will I tell him?"

"I'll be there!" Ichabod shouted. "I'll most certainly be there."

5

"All right, children," said the schoolmaster. "That'll be all for today. You can go home now. Run along."

The boys looked at each other in amaze-

"Run Along."

ment. The teacher never let them out early. He was more likely to make them stay late at school until they finished some boring lesson.

But not today. Today it was rush, rush, rush. He didn't even make them put their books away. And when they knocked over benches in their eagerness to leave, he didn't say a word. In a flash they were out of the school and running across the village green, shouting with joy and ready to have fun.

The gallant Ichabod was brushing and tidying up his best suit—actually, it was his only suit. He spent half an hour in front of a broken mirror that hung in the schoolhouse, slicking his hair and trying to look stylish.

Because he imagined himself a knight in shining armor, he decided that he must arrive at the Van Tassel party in style.

"I need to borrow a horse," he told the farmer he was staying with. "And, of course, a saddle."

His Best Suit

THE LEGEND OF SLEEPY HOLLOW

That ornery old Dutchman, Hans Van Ripper, looked at him through narrow eyes. "I guess you could take Gunpowder," Van Ripper said. "But you'll have to ride him with a firm hand. He's full of mischief, that horse. He has the devil in him."

Ichabod assured the farmer that he was a skillful rider, though in truth he'd only been on a horse a few times in his life. And so, sitting on this majestic mount, he rode out in quest of adventure.

"Let's go, Gunpowder," the schoolmaster said. The horse gave him a dirty look before he began to clomp slowly down the road.

Gunpowder was a broken-down work horse. He had the neck of a goat and a head like a hammer. His tail was all matted with burrs, and he was blind in one eye. But no matter how old and worn out he looked, he was a horse full of mischief.

"Onward, noble steed," Ichabod said to en-

"Onward, Noble Steed!"

courage the animal.

They made a good pair. Ichabod rode with short stirrups, so that his knees were up to the top of the saddle. His sharp elbows stuck out like grasshoppers'. He carried his whip upright, like a lance. As the horse jogged along, Ichabod's arms flapped like a pair of wings. The sight the horse and rider made as they shambled out of Van Ripper's gate was an odd one indeed.

It was a beautiful autumn evening. Frost had nipped the trees, turning their leaves to brilliant orange and purple and red. Wild ducks streamed past high in the sky, heading south. Squirrels scampered around gathering beech and hickory nuts for winter.

As usual, Ichabod's thoughts turned to food.

"What a lovely crop of apples this year," he said to himself. "Look at that great heap waiting for the cider press. And those pumpkins would make some tasty pies."

Upright, Like a Lance

Passing by some beehives, he couldn't help but think of a stack of steaming pancakes, and Katrina's dimpled little hand pouring honey over them.

It was quite a journey to the Van Tassel farm, all the way to the other side of Sleepy Hollow. Along the way Ichabod could see the peaceful waters of the Hudson reflecting distant mountains. By the time he approached the farm, the sun was setting in the west, turning the sky pink and gold.

"Why, what a crowd," Ichabod observed to his host. "Everyone in the region seems to be here tonight."

"Of course," said the jolly Master Van Tassel. "The more the merrier, we say. Have a good time, schoolmaster. Later we'll have dancing."

Ichabod looked around at the leather-faced farmers, with their homemade coats and huge shoes. Their wives wore plain country outfits that were very old-fashioned. The young ladies

"What a Crowd!"

might put on a fancy ribbon or straw hat they'd bought in the city. And the lads tied their hair back in short pony tails, which was the fashion of the time.

"Here comes Brom Bones!" someone shouted. Many of the party looked out to see him come thundering up on his magnificent horse, Daredevil. This was a horse, hardly even broken, who galloped with such wildness that he often came close to throwing his rider. Just the kind of animal Brom liked.

Ichabod didn't pay much attention to the entrance of his rival. He'd spied something that interested him more—and I don't mean all the pretty girls who were there that night. No, Ichabod had seen the food!

Platters were heaped with cakes that only Dutch housewives know how to bake. There were doughnuts and sweet cakes and shortbread.

"Help yourself, Master Crane," said Katri-

"Help Yourself, Master Crane!"

na's mother as she laid out more goodies.

"I don't know where to begin," Ichabod told her, though he'd already made a good beginning. "It all looks so good. Shall I have apple pie or peach pie or pumpkin pie?"

He decided a slice of each would be the best choice. He went on, piling his plate with ham and beef, with roast chicken and broiled fish and heaps of preserved peaches, plums, and pears. In fact, there wasn't a dish on the table that Ichabod didn't try.

"Delicious," he said, and took another mouthful. Nothing made him happier than eating. As he chewed, he rolled his eyes and chuckled to himself.

One day, he thought, this will all be mine. I'll snap my fingers in the face of Hans Van Ripper and all those stingy farmers. I'll be master of this house. No more school teaching then.

"Eat up," said old Baltus Van Tassel. "It's time for the dancing!"

"Delicious"

The fiddler was a gray-haired old man who'd been playing music in the region for fifty years. He ran his bow across his battered violin, nodding his head in time to the music. He stomped his foot every time a new couple were to start.

"May I have this dance?" Ichabod said to the lovely Katrina. He held his breath waiting for her answer.

"Certainly," she said. Ichabod's heart leapt with joy.

Ichabod prided himself on his dancing as much as on his singing. When he danced, his arms and legs shook, his head and hips rolled, every part of him moved to the music. His lanky body clattered around the room as if he were having a fit.

Tonight he was in bliss to be dancing with his sweetheart. He rolled his eyes at her, and she answered with smiles and winks.

All this time Brom Bones, jealous as he could be, sat in the corner by himself. He

Bliss To Be Dancing

brooded and frowned as he watched the dancers. The more Ichabod and Katrina whirled around the room, the more angry Brom Bones became.

6

When the dance was over, Ichabod joined Baltus Van Tassel and some of the older folks, who were sitting out on the porch talking about the Revolutionary War, which in those days was not long over. There had been fighting between the British and Americans near Sleepy Hollow. Everyone had a favorite story about what had happened to them.

"I almost captured a British warship all by myself," one old Dutchman said. "I would have, except my gun jammed."

"I blocked a musket ball with my sword," said another. When the others laughed, he offered to show them the dent in his sword as

Everyone Had a Favorite Story.

proof.

When each one had had a chance to tell what a hero he'd been in the war, the talk turned to ghosts. For these were people who lived near Sleepy Hollow. Everyone knew what strange and frightening things happened in that hidden spot.

"Have you ever seen the woman in white?" one old man asked. "She haunts the Hollow near Raven Rock. You'll hear her shriek on winter nights when a bad snow is coming. She died in an icy snowstorm years ago."

"The Headless Horseman has been out and about lately," said another man, puffing on his pipe. "I've seen him."

"As have I," another added. "He was riding past the old church on the hill."

"Did you hear," said Master Van Tassel, "what happened to old Brouwer?"

His friends said they had not.

"He never believed in spirits and such. But

"The Headless Horseman Has Been Out."

one night he was riding down that road by the glen where the trees grow so thick over the road that it's dark even during the day. The Horseman chased him over hill and dale until they reached the bridge that crosses the stream down there. At that point, the Horseman turned into a skeleton and flew over the trees with a clap of thunder. Old Brouwer tumbled head first into the stream."

The men nodded at this new tale, a lesson to those who don't believe.

"I met that silly Headless Horseman once," a voice said. They all looked. It was Brom Bones.

"I was riding home one night, when I saw him," he continued. "I offered to race him, bet I could beat him. And I would have. Daredevil can beat any horse—alive or dead. But just as we reached that bridge, the Horseman pulled up and vanished in a flash of fire."

Ichabod was impressed by these stories. He

Vanished in a Flash of Fire

added some of his own, telling what *he* had seen on his nightly walks through Sleepy Hollow.

Soon the time came for the party to break up. Farmers gathered up their families in their wagons and set out for home. You could hear them rattling through the quiet night as they went. Some of the girls went off with their boyfriends. Their laughter sounded fainter and fainter until it gradually died away.

The house grew quiet. Ichabod was the last to leave. He lingered to talk with Katrina, certain that he had won her heart.

We'll never know what she said to him. But she must have given him bad news, for he soon came out of the house looking as sad as any man ever looked.

Had the fickle Katrina been playing with him all along? Had she used him just to make Brom Bones jealous? Heaven only knows.

But her answer was written on Ichabod's

Ichabod Was the Last to Leave.

gloomy face. He trudged out to the barn to fetch his horse, who was sound asleep.

It was very late at night when Ichabod started on his somber journey home. The countryside, which had seemed so cheerful earlier, was now dark and dismal. The night was so still that he could hear a watch dog barking from all the way across the river.

Now all the stories of ghosts and goblins that he'd been hearing came back to him.

"My goodness, it sure is dark out tonight," he said to himself. Just then clouds moved in to cover the stars, and it grew darker still.

He was approaching the darkest, loneliest part of Sleepy Hollow. A man had been hanged from the big tree that stood beside the road. They said his ghost lingered there. As Ichabod drew closer, he began to whistle. And someone whistled back!

No, it was only the wind through some branches. For a moment he thought he saw

The Darkest, Loneliest Part of Sleepy Hollow

something white in the tree. But it proved to be a place where the wood had been split by lightning.

Suddenly he heard a groan. His teeth chattered in fright. But it was just two limbs of the tree rubbing against each other. Ichabod passed by. Nothing happened.

But up ahead, the road was even darker and spookier. He had to cross a little stream that everyone said was haunted. Nobody liked to cross that stream after dark. As Ichabod approached it, his heart began to thump.

"Come on, Gunpowder," he said. "Let's hurry up."

He gave the horse a few kicks in his ribs to make him move faster. But the horse would never do what his rider wanted. First he banged into a fence sideways. Then he plunged across the road into a bramble bush.

When he came to the stream, the stubborn horse stopped dead. Ichabod nearly went fly-

The Stubborn Horse Stopped Dead.

ing right over the animal's head.

As he righted himself in the saddle, the schoolmaster heard a sound. He peered into the darkness. Deep in a the shadow of a grove he was able to make out a black and towering shape. He couldn't see what it was, but he imagined it to be a gigantic monster ready to spring on him!

7

Ichabod's hair stood up on his head in terror. It was too later to turn and run. What should he do?

"Who—who are you?" he stammered.

The being did not reply.

"Who's there?" Ichabod repeated.

No answer. Ichabod nudged the stubborn Gunpowder into motion. He closed his eyes and began to sing one of his hymns.

A loud noise made him look around. The

A Black and Towering Shadow

creature had moved out to the middle of the road. Even in the darkness, Ichabod could see that it was a rider, an enormous figure on a powerful black horse. And he was following along behind the schoolmaster as he went.

"Giddy-up, Gunpowder," Ichabod said. "Let's go." He hurried on, hoping to leave the strange horseman behind. But the other kept pace with him.

Next, Ichabod tried slowing down to let the dark figure pass him by. But the stranger slowed down, too. Ichabod tried to sing his hymn again, but his mouth was so dry that he couldn't get a note out.

What he hated was the silence of the creature. It made not a sound, but rode along, mysterious and menacing.

They both went over a small hill. Now, viewing his fellow traveller against the background of the sky, Ichabod was horrified to see that the horseman had no head! Even worse, he

An Enormous Figure

was carrying the head, that should have been on his shoulders, in the crook of his arm!

Now Ichabod gave Gunpowder some fierce kicks to get him going. They galloped down the road as fast as the horse could run. But the specter came chasing right behind. Both of them were riding like the wind, throwing up stones and sparks as they went.

In his mad rush to get away, Ichabod paid little attention to where he was going. Now he discovered that Gunpowder had taken the road that led to the bridge so famous in all the ghost stories. It was the one just down the hill from the lonely churchyard where the Headless Horseman was said to be buried!

Gunpowder was running in a mad panic, and they actually managed to gain some distance on the awful pursuer. But just then Ichabod felt the girth come loose on his saddle!

He tried to hold onto it, but the saddle slipped and then fell off. The phantom horse

In a Mad Panic

behind them trampled it into the dust.

"Oh, no! Hans Van Ripper will be furious when he finds I've lost his good saddle," Ichabod gasped.

But he quickly realized that he had more terrible problems to worry about. One of them was trying to stay on Gunpowder's back. First he slipped to one side, then to the other. Sometimes he was jolted so hard on the horse's backbone, he thought he'd break in two.

But what was that up ahead? He saw starlight shimmering on a brook. He saw a church on a hill. And he saw a bridge. It was the same bridge where the Headless Horseman always disappeared!

"If I can just reach that bridge," thought Ichabod, "I am safe."

At that moment he heard the black steed panting close behind him. He imagined he could even feel the horse's hot breath.

"Go, Gunpowder, go!" he shouted. He gave

Panting Close Behind Him

the bony horse another kick.

Old Gunpowder sprang onto the bridge. His hooves thundered over the planks. As he reached the opposite side, Ichabod looked behind to watch the horseman vanish in a flash of fire just as he was supposed to.

Just at that moment he saw the goblin rise up in his stirrups and hurl his head at him. Ichabod tried to dodge the horrible missile, but too late. It crashed into his skull!

Ichabod tumbled into the dust. Gunpowder, the black steed, and the goblin rider passed by like a whirlwind.

The next day old Gunpowder was found without his saddle, munching grass by his master's gate. Ichabod did not appear for breakfast. Dinner hour came, but no Ichabod. The children showed up at school, but not their schoolmaster.

"What could have happened to Ichabod

Hurling His Head

Crane?" wondered Hans Van Ripper. "And where is my saddle?"

His neighbors helped him look. They found his saddle trampled in the dirt. They followed the tracks of horses' hooves leading to the bridge by the church. On the bank of the stream they found Ichabod's hat. Close beside it was a shattered pumpkin. They searched the brook, but did not find the schoolmaster's body.

Ichabod left only a few possessions behind, some clothes, a rusty razor, and a few books. In the back of a book about dreams and fortune telling were some sheets on which Ichabod had tried to write a poem to the fair Katrina. Hans Van Ripper burned these sheets and Ichabod's books along with them.

"I'll never send my children to school again," he swore. "No good comes of learning to read and write."

At church on Sunday, everyone was talking

A Shattered Pumpkin

of Ichabod Crane and his mysterious disappearance. Folks went down to the bridge to see where the cap and pumpkin were found. They talked over all the stories they'd heard. Finally they decided that Ichabod had been carried off by the Headless Horseman.

And with that, nobody troubled any more about the matter. They moved the school to another spot and hired a new schoolmaster.

Years later, an old farmer claimed that Ichabod Crane was still alive. The schoolmaster had moved to a distant part of the country and kept a schoolhouse there. He had studied law, had became a lawyer, had written for newspapers, and had even been elected judge.

Brom Bones, who soon after the disappearance married the lovely Katrina, always seemed to know something about the matter. Whenever anyone mentioned the pumpkin, he would burst into laughter.

But the old farmers' wives were the ones

Brom Bones Married Katrina.

who knew best. They were certain that Ichabod had been taken away by some spirit. They often told the story around the fire on a winter's night.

The deserted schoolhouse, they said, was haunted by the ghost of the poor teacher. A boy walking by there on a summer night would sometimes hear a distant voice singing a hymn, the sound drifting sadly through the quiet of Sleepy Hollow.

Haunted By the Ghost of the Teacher

"Out Shooting Squirrels"

Rip Van Winkle

1

"Rip Van Winkle!" The woman's voice boomed through the quiet village nestled at the foot of the hazy blue Catskill Mountains.

"Yes, my dear," a man answered, a little fearful of what his wife was going to say.

"Where have you been?" demanded the very cranky Dame Van Winkle.

"Why, out shooting squirrels in the mountains, my sweet," Rip said.

His wife was sour, not sweet, but Rip was always trying to butter her up.

"Show me the squirrels you shot for tonight's dinner," insisted Dame Van Winkle.

"I had no luck," Rip admitted. "The squirrels didn't come out to be shot today. But it was a lovely day for a ramble, all the same."

His wife frowned, her face so red it seemed about to explode like a volcano.

"It was a fine day for you to do your chores around this farm!" she screamed. "The chicken house needs whitewashing, the fence needs mending, the weeds need hoeing, and the ditches need clearing. And that's just the beginning."

Rip said nothing. He shrugged his shoulders, shook his head, and turned his eyes toward the sky.

This gesture always made his wife ten times as mad. She yelled at him till his ears hurt. He finally went outside.

His Wife Was Sour, Not Sweet.

"Shall I start with the chicken house?" he asked himself. "Or should I weed the garden first? Or should I fix that fence?"

Trying to decide which chore to tackle first, he wandered up to a meadow where there was a large elm tree. He sat down to think seriously about all the work he had to do. In a few minutes, weary from his ramble through the mountains, he was fast asleep.

You may think that Rip was lazy. But that wasn't true at all. He would sit on a wet rock for hours, holding a heavy fishing pole and never take a moment's rest. He would carry his musket through the woods and swamps all day. Up and down hills he would tramp, just to shoot one or two squirrels or a few wild pigeons.

"Rip," a neighbor would say, "could you help me build a stone wall on my farm?"

"Certainly," Rip would answer. He would pitch in and help till the sun went down. He

Up and Down Hills He Would Tramp.

was always there when anyone needed a hand to shuck corn or raise a barn or bring in some hay. He even helped out the women of the village, taking care of the little chores that their husbands never got around to.

It was only on his own little farm that he never seemed to get around to doing anything. But he had a reason.

"It's no use working on this piece of ground," he declared. "It's so barren and rocky, nothing will ever come of it, no matter what I do."

It was true the fences were always falling down. His cow would either go astray or break into the garden and eat the cabbages. Weeds grew better than any vegetable. Besides, whenever Rip was about to go out and get to work, it rained.

This farm he'd inherited from his father had dwindled until he had barely more than a patch of Indian corn and potatoes. And even that he couldn't keep up.

A Patch of Indian Corn and Potatoes

Rip could hardly support his family. His son, also named Rip, looked like his father, loved idleness like his father, and even wore his father's old clothes. He ran around town in a pair of pants so big he had to hold them up with one hand as he skipped after his mother.

Rip Junior loved his father, who played with him and his little sister and took them fishing. Rip was popular with all the children of the village. He would join in their games and make willow whistles for them. He never tired of taking them on his back and jogging around the village square.

Rip Van Winkle was a happy man. Take life easy, was his motto. He was as happy to eat white bread or brown, whichever he could get with the least effort. If left to himself he would have gladly whistled life away in perfect contentment. But his wife nagged him morning, noon, and night, to get to work

"I don't deserve such scolding," Rip would

Popular with All the Children of the Village

say when his wife couldn't hear him. "Do I, Wolf?"

Rip's best friend at home was his dog Wolf. They understood each other. Wolf was a brave dog, but he too was afraid of Dame Van Winkle. He would slink around the house with his tail between his legs, always watching his mistress with a cowardly eye. If she ever reached for a broom handle or a ladle, he would run out the door before she could beat him.

When Rip wanted to get away from his wife's bitter lectures, he strolled down to the town's small inn where all the wise men, philosophers, and other idle fellows met. Above them hung a portrait of His Majesty George the Third, King of England. At that time, America was still a colony of England.

"Did you hear about Yan Vanderscamp?" one of them would say. He would go on to relate some little bit of local gossip. Then somebody else would tell a story about nothing.

Rip's Best Friend Was His Dog.

Every so often a traveller would leave off an old newspaper. Derrick Van Bummel, the schoolmaster, would read them the latest news. He was an educated man, who could pronounce the most gigantic words in the dictionary.

When he finished, the men would have a deep discussion about world events, each offering his opinion about any topic you could think of.

The wisest of this group was the owner of the inn, Nicholas Vedder. He sat in his chair by the door all day, puffing on his pipe. Everyone respected his opinions even though he didn't say much. If he disagreed with something he smoked in short angry puffs. If he agreed, he let out peaceful clouds of smoke, or even took his pipe from his mouth and nodded his head.

One afternoon, Rip was discussing with his friends the best fishing spots on the streams

The Wisest Was Nicholas Vedder.

that flowed down from the mountains.

"That bend in the stream just past De Groot's woods is where you can catch the biggest trout," Rip was saying. "Just the other day I was fishing there and—"

"Rip," one of his pals said, interrupting him. "Here comes your wife."

"Rip Van Winkle!"

Rip heard the shrill tones of his wife's voice as she came storming down to the inn. He knew he was in for another scolding. He knew she would scream at his friends for encouraging his laziness. And what could he do but shrug and take it?

2

The only way Rip could get away from his wife's complaints, and away from the work of the farm, was to take his gun and stroll into the woods. He would carry a bit of lunch with

"Here Comes Your Wife!"

him and share his sandwich with Wolf.

"Poor Wolf," he said. "We both live a dog's life. But as long as I'm around, you'll always have a friend to stand by you."

Wolf wagged his tail and looked at his master as if to say, "I'll stand by you, too."

One fine autumn day, Rip rambled to one of the highest, most remote spots in the Catskill Mountains. All day he'd been trying to shoot squirrels, but without much luck.

He found himself on a green knoll looking out over a steep cliff.

"Look, Wolf," he said. "You can see the whole valley. Look at the shadows of the mountains beginning to stretch across the fields and forests. And there's the mighty Hudson River. What a sight!"

But this lovely view made him realize how far from home he was. It would be dark before he could get back to his village. He knew that Dame Van Winkle would be hopping mad

"What a Sight!"

when he returned.

"We'd better get going," he said to Wolf.

But as soon as they stood to head back, Rip heard a voice calling him from far off.

"Rip Van Winkle! Rip Van Winkle!"

He looked around, but could see nothing except a crow flying across the mountains. Maybe he was just imagining it.

But then he heard the words again in the still evening air. "Rip Van Winkle!"

Wolf gave a low growl and the hair stood up on his back. He crowded near his master and stared down into a glen.

Rip began to feel a little afraid. He looked down the hill and saw a strange figure toiling up the rocks. He was bending under the weight of something that he carried on his back.

Rip was surprised to see anyone in such a lonely place. But he was always eager to help someone in need, so he hurried down to the man.

A Strange Figure

The stranger's odd appearance surprised him. He was short, with a gray beard and bushy gray hair. He was dressed the way the old Dutchmen used to dress, in knee breeches that had rows of buttons down the side. On his back he was carrying what looked like a keg of liquor. He motioned Rip to approach.

"Can I give you a hand with your heavy load?" Rip asked.

The stranger said not a word, but signaled that he did indeed need help. So they took turns carrying the keg up a steep gully which looked like the dry bed of a stream. It was hard work.

As they went, Rip kept hearing thunder rolling down from the rocks above. He paused, then decided it must be just one of those passing thunderstorms that you often encounter in the mountains.

Up they went. The stranger remained completely silent. Rip was dying to ask him why

An Odd Appearance

he could possibly be lugging this heavy cask up the side of the mountain. But something about the odd little man made him hold his tongue.

Finally they passed through a ravine into a hollow that was surrounded by rock cliffs on all sides. Trees jutted out from the tops of the cliffs, casting the hollow into gloom. You could hardly see the sky.

"My goodness, Wolf," Rip said to his faithful dog, "look at those strange men!" He pointed.

Down in the center of the hollow, on a level piece of ground, a whole group of odd-looking men were bowling—playing ninepins, as they called it.

Like the man with the keg, they were dressed in old-fashioned Dutch outfits. They all had long knives at their belts. One had a broad face with the eyes of a pig. Another had an enormous nose. They all wore beards.

Their leader was a fat old man with the

Playing Ninepins

weather-beaten face of a sailor. He wore a broad leather belt, a high-topped hat, bright red stockings and thick-heeled shoes with roses on them.

"Why are they so silent?" Rip wondered to himself. For, though they should have been having fun, none of them said a word. Not one of them even smiled.

They didn't speak to each other, either. The only sound to break the stillness was the noise of the balls clattering into the pins, which echoed in the mountains like thunder.

When Rip and the little man approached them, they stopped bowling and gathered around. They stared at Rip without blinking. The coldness of their eyes made his heart miss a beat. His knees began to knock against each other.

The stranger who had been carrying the keg began pouring it into cups. He handed them to Rip to pass on to the others. Rip obeyed. He

His Heart Missed a Beat.

was afraid not to.

They drank in silence, then returned to their game of ninepins as solemn as ever.

"This is the oddest thing I've ever seen," Rip said to himself as he watched them play. "I guess I might as well have a taste of this drink myself. It can't do any harm."

Rip tasted the liquid and found it to be top notch. Since he was thirsty from lugging the keg up the mountain, he had another drink, and another.

It began to taste quite delicious. He drank until he grew quite tired. His eyes swam in his head. Finally his chin dropped to his chest and he fell into a deep sleep.

3

When he awoke, Rip found himself back on the green knoll where he'd first seen the odd little man. He rubbed his eyes—it was a bright

He Drank Until He Grew Tired.

sunny morning.

"Surely," thought Rip, "I haven't slept here all night."

He remembered what had happened before he fell asleep. There was the strange man with the keg, the climb up the ravine, the wild hollow among the rocks, and the weird group of little men playing ninepins.

"Oh, and that drink," Rip remembered. "That awful drink. What am I going to say to Dame Van Winkle when I get home? She'll be hopping mad."

He looked around for his gun. Lying beside him lay an old musket, the barrel rusted, the stock rotted. Rip always kept his gun clean and well-oiled.

"So," Rip said to himself. "Those strange men gave me a dose of drink, then robbed me of my gun. They left this piece of junk in its place. So that was their plan, Wolf."

But Wolf was nowhere to be seen. He must

An Old Musket

have run off after a squirrel. Or maybe the men had stolen him, too.

"Here, Wolf!" Rip called. He whistled. No dog came.

Rip decided to track down the men and demand his gun and dog back. Rising, he found his joints stiff. It hurt just to move.

"These mountain beds don't agree with me," he thought. "If this adventure makes me come down with a fit of the rheumatism, my wife will kill me."

He found the glen that he had walked up with the stranger. Yesterday it had been dry. Today he was surprised to find that a gushing mountain stream flowed down it. He had an awful time trying to make his way up the side of the torrent through brambles and vines.

He reached the spot where the ravine opened into the hollow. Surely this was where the men had played at bowling.

Yet now there was no opening, only a sheer

It Hurt Just To Move.

wall of rock. The stream came tumbling from above in a gushing waterfall. Rip couldn't figure it out.

"Here, Wolf!" he called again. He whistled for his dog.

"Caw, caw, caw!" came the answer. It was a crow, gliding high above, who seemed to mock Rip's troubles.

What should he do? It was late morning now and Rip was hungry for breakfast. He didn't want to leave his dog and gun behind. He surely didn't want to face his wife. But if he stayed in the mountains he'd starve.

Plenty worried, he took up the rusty old gun and headed home.

As he approached the village, he met a number of people. He didn't recognize any of them. That surprised him. He thought he knew everyone in those parts.

They wore unusual clothes, too. So many of them stroked their chins when they saw him

They Wore Unusual Clothes.

that Rip put his hand up to feel his own chin.

"Goodness," he said. "My beard has grown a foot long!"

In the village itself a group of strange children ran after him, laughing and pointing at his long gray beard.

"The town seems different," he thought. "There are more people around. And these rows of houses—I don't remember them being here yesterday."

Something very mysterious was going on. Maybe a sorcerer had cast a spell on the village. He wasn't in the wrong place. This *was* the town where he was born. Those *were* the Catskill Mountains. And over there was the stream he loved to fish in.

"It must be me," Rip told himself. "That drink last night shook up my poor head."

There was nothing to do now but to go home and face the anger of his wife. With each step he expected to hear the shrill voice of Dame

Laughing at His Long Gray Beard

Van Winkle.

When he arrived home he couldn't believe his eyes. His house had gone to ruin. The roof had fallen in. The windows were all shattered, the door off its hinges.

At least Wolf was there. Rip saw him skulking in the yard.

"Here, Wolf," Rip called, happy to find his old pal.

The half-starved dog looked at him and snarled, showing his teeth.

"My own dog has forgotten me," Rip sighed.

He entered the house, which his wife had always kept so tidy. It was a mess, empty and dirty. He forgot about being afraid of his wife and called her name. No one answered.

Rip hurried down to the inn to talk to his friends about these strange developments. But the inn was gone too. In its place was a large rickety building with a sign that said, "The

His House Had Gone to Ruin.

Union Hotel, Jonathan Doolittle, owner." Rip knew no one of that name.

Out front, where the big elm tree had stood, was a flag pole. The flag fluttering on top was a strange display of stars and stripes, which Rip had never seen before.

The picture of King George that always hung in front of the inn had changed too. The portrait there now showed a man in a blue coat and cocked hat holding a sword. Underneath, it said, GENERAL WASHINGTON.

"Who is this General Washington?" Rip wondered.

As usual, a crowd of people were gathered outside the building. Rip didn't recognize any of them. Nicholas Vedder wasn't there smoking his pipe. The schoolmaster Van Bummel was not sitting around reading stories from the newspaper.

The discussions going on were not the usual lazy talk that Rip remembered. Instead, a

The Inn Had Changed, Too.

skinny young man was talking about "elections," "congress," "liberty," "the Revolution"—things that made no sense at all to Rip.

When Rip appeared, with a troop of laughing children following him, the man stopped talking and everyone looked.

"Which side do you vote on, old man?" the speaker asked him.

Rip just stared. What was this stranger talking about?

"Are you a Federal or a Democrat?" asked another.

Rip didn't know what to say.

"You come to the election with a gun in your hand and a mob at your heels," declared another man. "Are you trying to start a riot?"

"Gentlemen," Rip said, "I am a poor quiet man, and a loyal subject of the king, God bless him!"

At these words, a great commotion broke out. On every side, people shouted, "A Tory! A

"A Loyal Subject of the King"

Tory! A spy! Arrest him!"

4

"Everybody quiet down," cried a self-important man in a cocked hat, who seemed to be in charge. He turned to Rip, looking very stern, and demanded, "Why do you come here and who are looking for?"

"I mean no harm," said Rip. "I only came to find some of my neighbors who always spend their time gathered in this spot."

"Neighbors? What neighbors? Name them."

"Well," Rip said, "where's Nicholas Vedder, who owns the inn?"

There was a silence. The men looked at each other, curious.

Finally, a very old man replied, "Nicholas Vedder has been dead for eighteen years. There used to be a wooden tombstone in the churchyard with his name on it, but now that's

"Dead for Eighteen Years"

rotten and gone too."

"Where is Brom Dutcher?" Rip asked, mentioning another of his friends.

"He went off to the army when the war began," someone told him. "Maybe he was shot or maybe he drowned, nobody knows. Anyway, he never came back."

"Where's Van Bummel, the schoolmaster?"

"He went to the wars too," was the reply. "He became a general in the militia. He's in Congress now."

Rip was very troubled to hear these answers. He felt all alone in the world. He couldn't understand how so much time could have passed. And what was this war they spoke of? And congress, what did that mean?

"Does nobody here know Rip Van Winkle?" he cried.

"Oh, Rip Van Winkle!" several people said. "Sure we know him. That's Rip Van Winkle over there, leaning against that tree."

He Felt All Alone.

Rip turned to see. The man who stood there was the spitting image of Rip himself the day he headed out to shoot squirrels in the mountain—just as lazy and just as ragged.

"Then that is me," Rip murmured. "Or, rather, I am—"

"Yes," said the man in the cocked hat, "who are you? What's your name?"

"God knows," Rip answered. "I'm not myself. I'm somebody else. That's me over there. I mean, no, that's somebody else in my shoes. Last night I was myself. I fell asleep on the mountain. They've changed my gun. They've changed everything. They've changed me. I can't tell you my name, or who I am!"

The bystanders began to wink at each other and tap their fingers against their heads as if to say, "The man is crazy."

"Maybe we should take his gun away before he hurts somebody," a man suggested.

At this point, a pretty woman with a baby

The Spitting Image of Rip Himself

in her arms pushed through the crowd to get a look at the man. The baby, frightened by Rip's wild appearance, began to cry.

"Hush, Rip," the mother said to her child. "This old man won't hurt you."

The name of the child and the face of his mother made Rip wonder.

"What's your name, good woman?" he asked.

"Judith Gardenier," she said.

"And your father's name?"

"Poor man, Rip Van Winkle was his name," she said. "But it's twenty years since he went away from home with his gun. He's never been heard from since. His dog came home without him. Whether he shot himself or was carried away by Indians, nobody knows. I was only a little girl then."

Rip had one more question to ask. His voice shook a little as he said, "Where's your mother?"

"Oh, she died too. Not long ago she got so

"His Dog Came Home Without Him."

mad at a New England peddler that she dropped dead."

Rip was a little relieved to hear this. Now he took his daughter up in his arms.

"I am your father!" he cried. "Young Rip Van Winkle once—Old Rip Van Winkle now! Does nobody know poor Rip Van Winkle?"

Everyone just looked at him, amazed. Finally an old lady tottered up and stared at Rip's face.

"Sure enough," she said. "It is Rip Van Winkle. Welcome home, old neighbor. Where have you been these twenty long years?"

Rip told his story. There wasn't much to tell. To him the twenty years seemed like one night.

The crowd of people winked at each other or put their tongues in their cheeks. Most shook their heads and smiled over the strange tale.

But one old Dutchman, the oldest man in the village, claimed that Rip's story made

"I Am Your Father."

sense.

"The Catskill Mountains have always been haunted by strange beings," he said. "Henry Hudson, who first sailed up this river that's named for him, comes back with his crew every twenty years to look after his discovery. My father saw them once playing ninepins in a hollow. And I have heard with my own ears the sound of their bowls, like distant peals of thunder."

There was an election on, so the crowd quickly lost interest in old Rip Van Winkle. His daughter took him home to live with her. She had a nice, well-furnished house. Rip remembered her cheerful farmer husband as one of the children who used to climb on his back.

Rip's son was hired to work on the farm. But, like his father, he paid little attention to his work. Most days he spent loafing or fishing or hunting squirrels.

Rip found some of his friends. But they were

His Daughter Took Him Home.

all old men now, and Rip preferred to make new friends among the young people.

He had nothing to do at home. He'd reached the age when a man is expected to retire and just sit around. That suited him fine. He sat happily in front of the inn all day with no one to bother him.

Those who gathered there liked to hear Rip's stories of the way things used to be "before the war." It took a while for him to understand that there had been a revolution. The country had broken away from England. And now he was a free citizen of the United States, not a subject of King George.

Rip didn't care much about politics, but he knew what it meant to be a free citizen. For he no longer had to put up with his wife's scolding and nagging. He could do just as he pleased, with not a single worry about Dame Van Winkle.

When somebody mentioned the poor

Sitting Happily in Front of the Inn

woman's name, he would shake his head, shrug his shoulders, and turn his eyes toward the sky. Whether he meant he was sad or happy, no one knew.

Every traveller who came to the hotel wanted to hear Rip's story. Soon everyone in the village knew it by heart. Some pretended that they didn't believe it. They insisted that Rip had gone crazy, and that this tale was just something he had imagined.

But the old Dutch people believed him. Even to this day, when a thunderstorm is heard on a summer afternoon rumbling down from the Catskills, folks will say, "It's Henry Hudson and his crew playing ninepins up in the mountains."

Every Traveller Wanted to Hear.

"Keep Out of My Garden!"

Golden Dreams

1

"Keep out of my garden!" Wolfert Webber yelled at the children who broke in to steal his cabbages. When he went back into his house, he told his wife, "The city's getting too big. Those pesky neighbor kids are always causing trouble."

It was the 1700s, a time when the mighty city of New York was only a small town on the tip of Manhattan Island. Wolfert and his wife lived on the outskirts. When his ancestors came to the new world, they brought with them the best cabbages in Europe. The family had raised cabbages for generations. Wolfert was famous for his cabbages.

At that time, the city was growing quickly. Houses were springing up everywhere. The rural lanes were becoming busy streets. All the noise and people bothered Wolfert. But even worse was the way the prosperous city seemed to make everybody rich except Wolfert. The cost of living went up, but he couldn't grow more cabbages than before. So he was always worrying.

"It wouldn't be so bad," he said to his wife, "if it was just the two of us. But we have to think of Amy."

The Webbers gave their daughter every advantage. She learned to sew very skillfully, and to put up all kinds of pickles and preserves. She liked to plant bright flowers among the cab-

"We Have to Think of Amy."

bages to make the garden more lovely.

Amy was a very pretty girl of 17. Like any growing girl, she wanted fine clothes and jewelry. Looking at the hearts pierced by arrows that she sewed into her hankies, Wolfert knew that she was interested in something more than planting flowers or putting up pickles.

This new interest was a young man named Dirk Waldron. He was the son of a poor widow, a strong and energetic youth with a fresh, clear face. He talked little, but he sat for long periods with the family. He filled Wolfert's pipe for him. He held the mother's ball of wool when she was knitting. He poured the tea and passed around the cups.

Though Amy was always giving Dirk sly glances and winks, her father never noticed. He sat by the fire smoking and worrying about money. But one night, as Amy was seeing Dirk to the door, her father heard the distinct smack of a kiss.

A Young Man Named Dirk Waldroon

"Can it be?" he asked himself. "My little girl has grown to become a woman. And what's worse, she's fallen in love."

Wolfert was a kind father, but a cautious one. Young Dirk had neither money nor land. If the two young people married, Wolfert would have to give them a corner of his farm. But the land was hardly enough to support Wolfert's own family. He figured it would be better to nip the romance in the bud. He went to his daughter and laid down the law.

"I don't want young Dirk Waldron in my house again," he told her. "I know how you feel, but this is for your own good."

Amy had a little cry over this. But because she was an obedient daugher she never pouted or sulked. From that time on, she wouldn't let Dirk into the house. If she talked to him, it was out the kitchen window or over the garden fence.

Wolfert's favorite place to pass the time was

"This Is for Your Own Good."

a country inn a few miles to the north, over by the river. It was an old Dutch tavern where he and his friends would gather to pitch horse-shoes and talk over business.

One bitter and windy autumn day, Wolfert walked up to the inn. Everyone was inside because of the cold. Since it was Saturday, there was a good crowd of folks sitting around talking.

"It will be a cold night for the money diggers," said the host.

"Are they at work again?" asked a one-eyed English army officer who always hung around the inn.

"Indeed they are," said the host. "And they've had good luck lately. They dug up a pot of gold behind Stuyvesant's orchard. It must have been buried there in the days of old Peter Stuyvesant, the Dutch governor."

"Fudge! I don't believe it at all," said the officer.

"You can believe it or not, just as you like,"

Friends Would Gather

said the host. "But everybody knows that Peter Stuyvesant buried a great heap of money when the English came to take over. Some say his ghost walks at night, looking just like the portrait of him."

"I still say fudge!" said the one-eyed officer.

"Well, Corney Van Zandt saw him," said the host. "Out at midnight he was, walking around on his wooden leg, and with a sword in his hand that flashed like fire. Why would a ghost be walking except that somebody was digging near his buried treasure?"

Wolfert Webber listened very carefully to these words. Whenever the talk turned to treasure, he always perked up his ears. He sure wanted to find some of that buried gold for himself.

2

The next to speak was an old man named

"His Ghost Walks at Midnight."

GOLDEN DREAMS

Peechy Pauw Van Hook. He knew more stories than anyone at the inn, and he was always eager to tell one.

"Folks have dug up money in many parts of this here island," he declared. "They always dream three times about treasure before they find it. It's usually a heap of money the old Dutchmen buried years ago."

"Fiddlesticks with your Dutchmen!" cried the English officer. "All this treasure was buried by Captain Kidd and his crew."

He began to tell stories about Captain Kidd, the greatest pirate that ever sailed the seas. The tales always ended with the buccaneer burying his loot in some hidden spot right there on the island of Manhattan.

Wolfert Webber took all this in. As he was walking home, he couldn't help but imagine the great quantities of treasure buried around him. Why, he might be walking on top of a pile of gold right this minute.

Burying His Loot

"Why am I so unlucky?" he asked himself. "Others go to bed and dream of wealth. The next morning they go out and dig up gold doubloons as if they were potatoes. But I dream only of my troubles. And all I dig is cabbages."

He went to bed that night feeling very low. But as soon as he was asleep, he dreamed of a huge treasure buried in his garden. Every time he thrust in the shovel, he turned up more gold, diamonds, and sacks of money.

When he awoke, he was as poor as ever. He didn't even want to work in his fields. He only sat by the chimney and thought about buried treasure.

The next night, he dreamed of gold again. He passed the day wishing that his dream would come true.

The third night, he could hardly sleep. But sure enough, as soon as he dozed off, the golden dream came to him again.

"A dream repeated three times has never

He Dreamed of a Huge Treasure.

been known to lie," he declared the next morning.

He was so excited he put his shirt on backwards. He was rich! All he had to do was to dig up the treasure buried beneath his cabbage field.

At breakfast, he asked Amy to put a lump of gold in his tea! Passing the pancakes to his wife, he told her to help herself to a gold doubloon!

The problem was, how could he uncover the treasure without anyone knowing? He would dig at night!

Every night he was out in his fields with a pick and shovel, digging as fast as he could by the light of a lantern. Up and down his fields he went, searching for the treasure. Soon his orderly fields of cabbage began to look like a battlefield.

"You're digging up all the cabbages!" his wife pleaded with him.

Digging as Fast as He Could

GOLDEN DREAMS

"You're ruining my flowers!" his daughter cried.

"It doesn't matter," Wolfert assured them. "Soon we'll all be rich. Rich!"

His family began to think that Wolfert had gone crazy. Even in his sleep he talked about gold and pearls and diamonds. During the day he walked around as if in a trance.

Dame Webber went to her friends to tell them the latest foolishness of her husband. And Amy couldn't concentrate on her sewing, worry as she did about her father.

"Cheer up," Wolfert told her. "Some day we'll be as rich as the Van Horns and the Van Dams. Why, the governor himself will be glad to have his son marry you."

Amy just shook her head.

Wolfert went on digging. His dream had not told him exactly where to find the treasure. Because his cabbage fields were large, he had to try everywhere. He dug and dug, but he still

"You're Ruining My Flowers!"

had a long way to go when winter set in.

The ground froze hard and it was too cold at night to dig. But as soon as frogs announced that spring had returned, Wolfert was right back out there digging.

He no longer worked during the day; he just sat around. At night he went into the fields and dug hole after hole. He found nothing. Instead of growing rich, he neglected his crops and became poorer than ever.

All summer he dug for treasure. Before he knew it, another autumn came. He still hadn't found any gold.

When the cold weather arrived again, he didn't have his usual supply of cabbages. His family had to scrimp to get by.

"What could be worse," he asked, "than to have to pinch pennies when a fortune in treasure lies buried out in your own field?" Feeling terrible, he moped around and worried all the time.

His Family Had to Scrimp.

At first, his neighbors thought poor Wolfert had gone crazy, so they all pitied him. But then word went around that Wolfert was broke, so they all avoided him.

The only one who continued to come around was Dirk Waldron. He was still in love with Amy, and she still smiled at him from the kitchen window. He seemed to love her even more now that she was truly poor.

3

Many months had passed since Wolfert had visited the country inn where he used to spend his time. One Saturday afternoon, feeling very sorry for himself, he was taking a long walk and found himself near the inn.

He wondered whether he should enter. His friends didn't seem to want to see him anymore. But he needed to talk to somebody, so he went in through the door.

Still in Love With Amy

GOLDEN DREAMS

His old pals were all there, along with a stranger who immediately drew Wolfert's attention. This newcomer had the weather-beaten features of a sailor. His face bore a long scar across the cheek that split his upper lip and let his teeth show through. He talked in a loud voice and ordered everyone around.

"You're wondering who that stranger is," said Peechy Pauw, taking Wolfert aside. "It's an odd story."

Several months earlier, during a fierce storm, this man had landed on the shore with his enormous sea chest. He took a room at the inn and had lived there ever since. He spent much of his time sitting by the window and looking out at the water through a telescope. He watched every ship that came by.

"You should hear the stories he tells," Peechy Pauw whispered to Wolfert. "He knows about every pirate adventure of the last twenty years. He loves to tell about terrific fights

He Watched Every Ship.

over Spanish galleons full of treasure!"

No one dared to contradict the sailor. If they did, he would shout, "How do you know? Were you there?"

In fact, many of the men who gathered at the inn began to wonder if these were stories the stranger heard, or if he actually *was* a pirate. Maybe he had helped raid the ships he talked about. Maybe he had taken part in the fierce fights himself. The owner of the inn wanted to get rid of the stranger, but he didn't know how.

Wolfert was amazed to hear of the arrival of this strange man. He was also eager for any new account of pirate treasure. He took a seat where he could listen to everything that was being said in the room. Sure enough, the sailor soon began to tell of the capture of a Spanish cargo ship by pirates.

"There was a terrible fight," he said. "A few of the pirates were shot. But they kept coming

Listening to Everything

at the ship's crew, clanking their swords something fierce. They took over the ship. But a Spanish gentleman who was aboard would not give up. He gave the pirate captain an awful sword slash right across his face."

"What did they do with the prisoners?" Peechy Pauw asked.

"Threw them all overboard!" the sailor answered with a wicked grin.

Dead silence followed these words. All the honest townsmen looked at the deep scar that ran across the stranger's face. They moved nervously in their chairs.

The one-eyed army officer was always trying to top the stranger's stories. He now began a long account of Captain Kidd and his crew.

"And when they had the treasure in their hands," he said, finishing the story, "they sailed up the Hudson and buried it on this island."

"Threw Them All Overboard!"

"Never!" shouted the sailor. "Kidd never came up the Hudson to bury any treasure."

"I tell you he did!" insisted the officer.

"And what do you know about it anyway?" the sailor demanded.

"I was in London when Captain Kidd was tried as a pirate," said the officer. "I saw him hanged."

"They should have hanged a landlubber instead," was the reply of the sailor.

The officer had no answer to this. He fell silent, staring bitterly at the stranger.

"I have to agee," said Peechy Pauw, "that Captain Kidd never buried any money around here. But there were plenty of pirates that used to pull into the little coves along Manhattan Island and hide their loot. Why, I remember one time—"

He was interrupted by the sailor slamming his fist on the table.

"Hark ye!" the man said. "You'd better let

Slamming His Fist

the buccaneers and their treasure alone. They fought hard for their money. You landlubbers shouldn't be thinking about digging it up, if you want to stay out of trouble."

Peechy Pauw held his tongue. Silence fell on the room. The sailor pulled out a Spanish-looking watch, checked the time, and went up to his room.

Wolfert Webber had been listening carefully to this talk of pirates. All of the stories were full of gold and diamonds and shiny doubloons. And the stranger, Wolfert thought, had to be a pirate himself. He would surely know the truth about buried treasure.

4

After the sailor went up to his room, everyone urged Peechy Pauw to continue his story. A thunderstorm had blown up outside and because of the rain no one wanted to start for

"Let the Buccaneers and Their Treasure Alone."

home until the storm passed.

"Everybody knows Old Sam," Peechy began. "He's the old black man who's been fishing around this island for a good fifty years. One evening, when he was still a young man, he was trying his luck up in the area of Hell Gate."

According to the story, Sam was concentrating so hard on his fishing that he didn't notice that the tide had changed. The currents and whirlpools were so dangerous around those parts, that he had to wait until the tide changed again before he could row home.

As night came on, a storm swept in from the west. Sam pulled his boat into a cove along the Manhattan shore. He tied up under a tree. Protected by a canopy of leaves, he waited as the wind roared and lightning flashed. He settled in the bottom of his boat and fell asleep.

When he awoke, the storm had passed and

Protected By a Canopy of Leaves

all was quiet. The night was very dark. Sam started to untie his boat when he saw a light approaching rapidly across the water. It was a lantern in the bow of a boat.

"This is the place," he heard a voice say. "Here's the iron ring."

The boat was tied up in the little cove very near to where Sam was. Five desperate-looking fellows came ashore carrying something heavy. Some of them were armed with knives and pistols. They carried their load into the bushes.

Curious, Sam crept out of his boat and climbed a ridge above where the men were headed.

"Have you brought the spades?" one man asked.

"They're here," said another. "We must dig deep so that no one finds it."

A cold chill ran through Sam's veins. They must be murderers about to bury their victim.

Five Desperate-Looking Characters

Now, Sam loved a mystery. Instead of sneaking back to his boat, he decided to creep even closer. He moved inch by inch, careful not to make any noise. Soon he reached a large rock. When he raised his head above the edge of it, he found that he was right above where the men were digging. He froze, terrified of making the least sound.

By this time, the grave was nearly filled back in. The men replaced the turf and scattered leaves over it so that no one would notice that the ground had been dug.

"Not even the devil himself will find it now," one man said.

"You murderers!" Sam shouted without thinking.

All the men looked up to where Sam was peeking over the rock.

"Get him!" one shouted.

Sam heard a pistol being cocked, but he was already running. He scrambled through the

"Get Him!"

brush as fast as he could go. He could hear the murderers chasing after him.

Soon he came to the edge of the cliff that overlooked the cove where he had left his boat. It was a sheer drop—he could go no farther. One of the men saw him up there. He aimed his pistol and fired.

The bullet went whistling past Sam's head. But Sam was smart enough to give a yell and fall down. He pushed a big rock over the cliff. It splashed in the water.

"That's the end of him," the man told his pals. "He'll tell no tales, except to the fish."

Sam now snuck down to the water's edge and climbed quietly into his boat. He cast off, letting the current take him down the river a way before he dared to row. Then he made his way home as fast as he could. He didn't feel safe until he was back in his own bed.

Here, Peechy Pauw ended his story and took a drink.

Chasing After Him

"Is that all?" asked the one-eyed officer. "Didn't Sam ever find out what it was they buried?"

"That's all. Sam wasn't so eager to go back there. Why would he look for a dead body when the murderers were long gone?"

"But are you sure it was a dead body they were burying?" asked Wolfert. He had already convinced himself that it was a fortune in gold.

"I'm sure," said Peechy. "It still haunts that ruin of a house that sits not far from Hell Gate."

"That's all fudge!" said the officer. "It's nothing but an old wives' tale."

"Indeed it is not," Peechy declared. "I believe it as well as if it had happened to me."

Wolfert didn't say anything more. But his head was full of gold doubloons. That was what those pirates had buried and he knew it. He was already thinking of some way to find

His Head Was Full of Gold Doubloons.

the spot. Then he could simply dig up the treasure, and he'd be rich.

There was a brief silence. The storm, for the moment, had calmed.

Then from outside, the men all heard the loud crack of a musket being fired. They rushed to the window. From down by the water they heard someone yell. Then another musket shot.

What could it mean?

5

"Ahoy, there!" cried the strange sailor from his room on the second floor. He had flung his window open. The men downstairs could hear him shouting into the night.

Someone answered. His voice seemed to be coming from out on the river itself. But when lightning flashed across the sky, no one could be seen.

The Crack of a Musket

They heard a loud boom and then a scraping sound overhead, as if someone was moving furniture. The sailor called for a servant to come and help him.

A few minutes later he appeared downstairs. Aided by the servant, he was carrying his big sea chest.

The owner of the inn was amazed. "Surely you are not going on the water in the middle of a storm like this," he said.

"Storm!" the sailor scoffed. "Do you call such a sputter of weather a storm?"

"You'll get drenched to the skin and catch your death of cold," said Peechy Pauw.

"Thunder and lightning!" said the sailor. "Don't preach about weather to a man who has sailed in hurricanes."

They heard the voice from out on the water calling again. The sailor, with the help of the servant, lugged his heavy sea chest out of the inn and down toward the shore.

Carrying His Big Sea Chest

GOLDEN DREAMS

They couldn't believe he was actually going to go out onto the wild waves in this storm. They went out with a lantern to follow him down.

"Get rid of that light!" cried a hoarse voice from the water. "No one wants lights here!"

"Thunder and lightning!" yelled the sailor. "Get back to the inn, all of you! You have no business following me!"

Wolfert and his friends took a few steps backward. Curious to see what happened, they watched from the bushes. A flash of lightning showed a boat full of men near the point. It rose and sank with each wave. The men could barely keep hold of the shore with a long pole.

The sailor rested one end of the sea chest on the edge of the boat and grabbed the handle to lift it in. Just then the boat was jerked away from the shore by a wave. The chest splashed into the water, pulling the sailor with it. Both

"You Have No Business Following Me!"

of them quickly sank out of sight.

"Look out!" the men on shore shouted. The boat was pulled away by the current.

Wolfert thought he heard a cry for help. But when the next lightning flash came, the water where the sailor had fallen in was empty and the boat was gone. Only the waves kept splashing against the rocks.

The men returned to the inn, badly shaken by what they had seen.

"At least he paid his bill before he left," said the owner of the inn.

"He came in a storm and went in a storm," said Peechy Pauw. "Nobody knows where he came from, nobody knows where he went to."

"He's gone to Davy Jones' locker," said Wolfert.

The storm that had raged around the inn now ended. It was almost midnight, so all the men set out for home. As they left, each gave a nervous glance toward the shore where the

The Boat Was Gone.

sailor had disappeared. Wolfert half expected to see him there, floating on his sea chest in the moonlight.

He couldn't stop thinking of the account of Old Sam. He was sure he knew the real story. The men in the boat weren't murderers, they were pirates. They'd come to bury their treasure. That treasure still lay somewhere waiting to be uncovered.

Wolfert finally saw a sure way to find the treasure for which he'd been searching during all those long years. He would get Old Sam to lead him to the place of his adventure and point out the exact spot. Then he would dig up the gold and be rich for the rest of his life.

Wolfert could hardly wait. He had to find Old Sam!

"I've fished these waters since before you were born," Sam said, when Wolfert finally found him. "The event you're talking about

He Had to Find Old Sam.

happened a good long time ago."

Sam lived down at the tip of Manhattan, near what's now the Battery. He'd built his small cabin from driftwood and pieces of wrecked ships near the old fort there.

Wolfert got him to tell the story of the night the men buried something up along the shore.

"Nobody's uncovered what those men buried, have they?" Wolfert asked.

"I wouldn't know about that," said Sam. "I do know there's a lot of crazy people around. They spend their time digging for gold when they could be fishing."

Sam was an old man now, with white hair on his head. Wolfert promised to pay him handsomely if he would guide him back to the very spot where his adventure had occurred. Sam was glad to do it.

"We can't go right now," Sam said. "The tide's not right."

"We'll walk," Wolfert said. He was so anx-

Wolfert Got Him to Tell the Story.

ious to get his gold, he didn't want to wait a minute.

They walked about five miles up the eastern shore of Manhattan. They made their way through overgrown brush and brambles until they came to a spot where a house had once stood. Now it was just a pile of rubble with two chimneys still standing.

"This," thought Wolfert, "is that silly haunted house they talk about."

The two men walked down to the water's edge. Sam pointed out the cove where the men had landed. An iron ring was still fixed in the rock. Above it, three small crosses were carved into the stone face.

It took more searching to find the place of the burial. It had been night when Sam first came there, and he'd been more interested in what the men were doing than in where they did it.

They finally came to a spot which Sam

Three Small Crosses

thought was right.

"Look!" Wolfert exclaimed. "There are the same three crosses carved into the rock. Probably left there as a sign. Now, tell me, where did the men dig?"

"I'm not altogether sure about that," Sam said. "Maybe it was over there. Or it could have been by that mulberry bush, or it might have been up on that knoll."

"Well, it's too late to start digging now," said Wolfert. "Anyway, we didn't bring shovels. We'll have to come back."

The two men started for home. When they were passing the old farm, a noise caught their attention. They looked around to see a man carrying a sack toward the ruined house.

"Oh, my!" Wolfert exclaimed. "It's the sailer from the inn, the same who drowned in the river the other night."

At that point, the sailor turned and waved his fist at Wolfert as if to threaten him.

Carrying a Sack

Wolfert didn't stay around to see anything more. He and Sam both ran. They tore through the brush and didn't slow down until they reached the road back to town.

Now Wolfert wasn't so sure he wanted to return to that haunted spot. He wandered around his house all day, dreaming of gold and also of the mysterious sailor's ghost. He talked in his sleep and was bothered by nightmares.

His wife decided to call in Doctor Kipper. He was famous in Manhattan not just for his healing skills, but because he knew all about witchcraft and magic.

"He's not been himself for a long time, Doctor," Dame Webber said. "Can't you please do something?"

Dr. Kipper listened carefully as the woman described her husband's behavior. He was especially interested in Wolfert's search for gold.

The truth was, that Dr. Kipper was also

Doctor Kipper

eager to get rich by digging for buried treasure. So instead of curing Wolfert of his obses-
sion with digging, he caught the same illness
himself.

"I'm sure you're right about the money being
buried out there," the doctor told Wolfert. "But
you must uncover it carefully and with much
secrecy. You especially need to have a divining
rod."

"Where would I get one of those?" Wolfert
asked.

"Perhaps I could find such a thing for you,"
Dr. Kipper said. "I would like to help you all I
can."

This was wonderful. Wolfert was glad to
have an educated man to help him look for the
treasure.

Dame Webber was pleased that the doctor's
visits seemed to be helping her husband im-
mensely. Little did she know that the two men
were busy making plans to go out together and

Eager to Get Rich

hunt for buried gold.

6

"Now, I don't want you to worry," Wolfert told his wife when the night came for him to go off on his adventure. "I might not return until morning."

Of course, this news *did* make her worry. She and Amy both begged Wolfert not to go. But nothing could stop him. He set out under a starlit sky. He and Dr. Kipper met Sam at the shore and soon they were all rowing up the river.

"Did you hear something?" Wolfert asked the others.

"What is it?" the doctor replied.

"It sounded like someone rowing after us," said Wolfert.

They did hear the low sounds of oars. Sam rowed faster. The sounds disappeared behind

All Rowing Up the River

them.

Soon they arrived at the cove and tied the boat to the iron ring. They moved as quietly as they could. Every noise made them start.

"This is the place," Wolfert said. "There are the three crosses."

While Wolfert held the lantern, the doctor walked around with the divining rod, which was just a forked twig. At first nothing happened. Then, like magic, the rod began to turn in the doctor's hands. It dropped down until it was pointing toward the earth.

"This is the exact spot!" Dr. Kipper whispered.

"Shall I dig?" Wolfert asked.

"No, of course not! We must complete the ceremonies to drive away evil spirits."

The doctor drew a circle for all three of them to stand in. He started a fire with some twigs. The herbs that he burned sent up smoke that made Wolfert sneeze. The doctor read some

"This Is the Exact Spot!"

words from a book, then said it was time to dig.

Sam began to dig with the spade. For a long time he threw sand and gravel out of the hole. Wolfert leaned over, holding the lantern, looking for the first glimmer of gold.

But the digging went on and on. The hole grew deeper and deeper. They uncovered nothing but rocks.

All of a sudden the spade hit something hollow.

"It's a chest," Sam said.

"Full of gold!" Wolfert said. He'd never been so happy.

No sooner had he spoken than all three men heard a noise above them. Wolfert turned. Peeking over a rock was the terrible scarred face of the drowned sailor!

Wolfert dropped the lantern, and it went out. In the darkness, the three men ran in three different directions. Wolfert crashed

"It's a Chest!"

through the bushes. He heard someone chasing right behind him. He ran faster, but could not escape.

In a minute he found himself on a cliff overlooking the river. A hand grabbed him. He turned and began to struggle with someone. It was too dark to see who it was.

Suddenly another man loomed out of the shadows and grabbed Wolfert's pursuer. Now these two men wrestled with each other. Wolfert couldn't escape because he was right on the edge of the cliff.

One of the two men sent the other flying over the edge. Wolfert heard him splash into the water below. Now the other was coming at him. All he could see was the shape of a human figure. There was nowhere to escape.

"Keep away!" Wolfert cried. He began to climb down the steep slope.

The next minute, he slipped. He tumbled downward, bouncing from rock to rock and

He Began to Struggle.

bush to bush.

When Wolfert awoke, the light of dawn was seeping into the sky. He found himself lying in the bottom of a boat. He was too sore and stiff to even look around.

"Lie still, Master Webber," a voice said.

Wolfert knew that voice. It was Dirk Waldron, his daughter's suitor.

"Your wife begged me to follow you," Dirk explained. "She was afraid of what might happen. But I had a hard time keeping up. I only arrived in time to rescue you from your attacker—whoever it was."

So instead of going home loaded with treasure, Wolfert had to be carried on a board, with nothing to show for his trouble. When they heard his story, some of the townspeople went back to the scene of the digging. They found nothing.

To this day, the secret has never been revealed. Was there ever really treasure there?

"Lie Still, Master Webber."

Did someone else find it? No one knows.

Wolfert was in no condition to worry about treasure or pirates or anything else. He lay sick in bed, tended to by his wife and daughter. They bound up his wounds and sat at his bedside from morning to night.

All of Wolfert's old friends came around to wish him well. Many brought herbs and different kinds of tea they said would help him to recover. Dirk Waldron came by every day to cheer him up.

Nothing did any good. Wolfert grew weaker and weaker. He could do nothing but groan and sigh. To make matters worse, he learned that a new street was being planned. It would go right through the middle of his cabbage fields.

"That will complete my ruin," he moaned. "Now what will become of my daughter?"

"Leave Amy to me," Dirk answered. "I'll take good care of her."

Sick in Bed

Wolfert looked up at the strong, handsome young man. He knew this was the man for his daughter to marry.

"You have my blessing," he said. "Now call a lawyer so that I can make my will. I don't have long to live."

The lawyer arrived. Everyone was very sad to think these were Wolfert Webber's final hours. Amy cried by her father's bedside. Dame Webber took up her knitting to hide her grief.

"Write my will quickly," Wolfert said. "I can feel my end approaching."

The lawyer spead out a piece of paper and prepared to write.

"I leave behind my entire farm—" Wolfert began faintly.

"Do you mean those fields that the town is going to run a main street through?" the lawyer asked him.

"That's right," Wolfert said, sinking back on

"Write My Will, Quickly!"

his pillow.

"Well, whoever inherits that piece of ground will become one of the richest people in these parts," the lawyer said.

A glimmer of light appeared in Wolfert's eyes.

"You don't say!" he said.

"I do say. When those fields are cut into building lots, whoever owns them will be very, very wealthy."

"Really?" Wolfert said. "Then I think I will not make out my will just yet."

From that moment, Wolfert began to get better. In a few days he left his room. Soon he was making plans for streets and preparing deeds for building lots.

The lawyer, instead of helping him make his will, helped him to make a fortune. Houses were built all over his fields, and from then on, instead of cabbages, Wolfert harvested money.

He added on to his own house until it was

"You Don't Say!"

the biggest in the neighborhood. And soon it was filled with many chubby-faced grandchildren.

Wolfert Webber's golden dreams had finally come true.

The Biggest in the Neighborhood